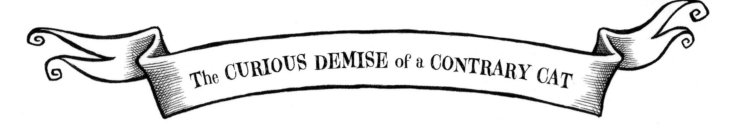

The CURIOUS DEMISE of a CONTRARY CAT

Story by **Lynne Berry**

Pictures by **Luke LaMarca**

Simon & Schuster Books for Young Readers

New York   London   Toronto   Sydney

SIMON & SCHUSTER BOOKS FOR YOUNG READERS

An imprint of Simon & Schuster Children's Publishing Division

1230 Avenue of the Americas, New York, New York 10020

Text copyright © 2006 by Lynne Berry

Illustrations copyright © 2006 by Luke LaMarca

All rights reserved, including the right of reproduction in whole or in part in any form.

SIMON & SCHUSTER BOOKS FOR YOUNG READERS is a trademark of Simon & Schuster, Inc.

Book design by Einav Aviram and Dan Potash

The text for this book is set in Hombre.

The illustrations for this book are rendered in pen and ink.

Manufactured in China

2 4 6 8 10 9 7 5 3 1

CIP data for this book is available from the Library of Congress.

ISBN-13: 978-1-4169-0211-9

ISBN-10: 1-4169-0211-2

To John—L. B.
For Mom & Dad—L. L.

On a pale gray night with a bright full moon, Witch was dressing for a bash.

"Cat," said Witch, "fetch me a hat!"
But Cat was busy, chasing Rat.

"Cat?" said Witch.

"Purr?" said Cat.

"Hat!" said Witch.

"GRRRRR," said Cat.

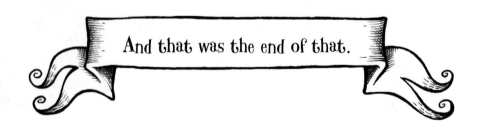

And that was the end of that.

Witch got her own hat. "DRAT THAT CAT!"

On a pale gray night with a bright full moon, Witch was greeting Ghost and Bat.

"Cat," said Witch, "fetch me a chair!"
But Cat was busy, eyeing Bat.

"Cat?" said Witch.

"*Purr?*" said Cat.

"Chair!" said Witch.

"*GRRRRR,*" said Cat.

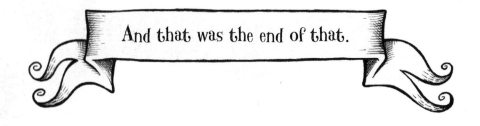

And that was the end of that.

On a pale gray night with a bright full moon, Witch was serving punch and pie.

"Cat," said Witch, "fetch me a cup!"
But Cat was busy, stalking Ghost.

"Cat?" said Witch.

"*Purr?*" said Cat.

"CUP!" said Witch.

"*GRRRRR,*" said Cat.

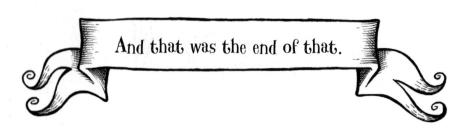

And that was the end of that.

On a pale gray night with a bright full moon, Witch was wishing for a jig.

"Cat," said Witch, "fetch me a fife!"
But Cat was busy, chasing Troll.

"Cat?" said Witch.

"*Purr?*" said Cat.

"**FIFE!**" said Witch.

"*GRRRRR,*" said Cat.

And that was the end of that.

Witch got her own fife. "DRAT THAT CAT!"

"But shall we dance, my Spooks and Sprite?"

On a pale gray night with a bright full moon, Witch was bidding guests good-bye.

"Cat," said Witch, "fetch me a cloak!"
But Cat was busy, spooking Sprite.

"Cat?" said Witch.

"Purr?" said Cat.

"CLOAK!" said Witch.

"GRRRRR," said Cat.

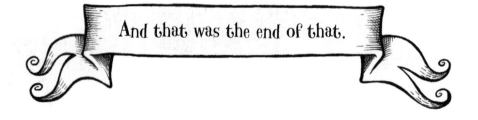

And that was the end of that.

Witch got her own cloak. "DRAT THAT CAT!"

"But let me see you out, dear Gnomes."

On a pale gray night with a bright full moon, Witch was cleaning cups and crumbs.

"Cat," said Witch, "fetch me a broom!"
But Cat was back to chasing Rat.

"Cat?" said Witch.

"Purr?" said Cat.

"BROOM!" said Witch.

"GRRRRR," said Cat.

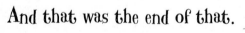 And that was the end of that.

Witch got her own broom. "DRAT THAT CAT!"

On a pale gray night with a bright full moon, Witch was brewing one last spell.

"Cat," said Witch, "fetch me a toad!"
But Cat was snoozing on the mat.

"Cat?" said Witch.

"Purr?" said Cat.

"TOAD!!!" cried Witch.

"GRRR—
—rribbit?"

And **THAT** was the end of Cat.